THE OFFICIAL

RAINBOW
HIGH™
YEARBOOK

HARPER
An Imprint of HarperCollinsPublishers

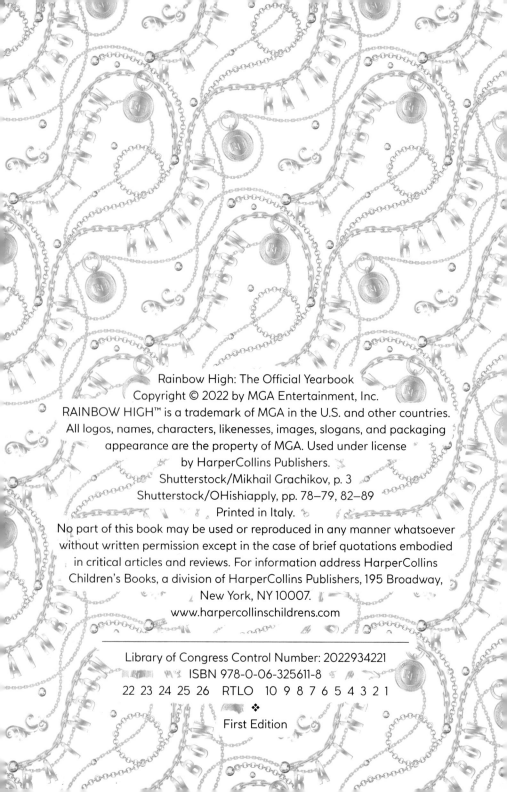

Library of Congress Control Number: 2022934221
ISBN 978-0-06-325611-8
22 23 24 25 26   RTLO   10 9 8 7 6 5 4 3 2 1
❖
First Edition

FROM MS. WRIGHT

Rainbow high prides itself on challenging our students to rise to every occasion. This past year, our students have not only demonstrated outside-the-box thinking, but they have taken it to a whole new dimension. This year was truly a change in perspective for us all!

As you know, our goal is to teach the virtues of G.L.A.M.: Grit, Love, Action, and Moxie, and I am proud of all our students who have demonstrated those virtues when facing the challenges of this past year.

Lou Wright

Ms. Lou Wright, Headmistress

RUBY ANDERSON

RUBY is a style trailblazer and her looks are totally fire! She designs fashion-forward, sporty glam looks for all occasions with a street-art vibe and is known for her custom kicks and super-cool hats.

FOCUS:
Mixed Media

RUBY
RH
MIXED MEDIA FOCUS

#FIRE RUBY HAS HER OWN ONLINE STORE AND HER TOP SELLER IS SNEAKERS.

#DYK WHEN SHE'S NOT MAKING ART, SHE LOVES DOING JIGSAW PUZZLES WITH EMI AT THE RAINBOW UNION.

#GOALS SHE GETS INSPIRATION FROM FAMOUS LUXURY BRANDS AND ADDS HER OWN SPECIAL TOUCH TO HER DESIGNS.

#FYI RUBY CONSIDERS HER ART FORM MIXED MEDIA, BECAUSE SHE USES DIFFERENT MATERIALS AND CANVASES TO EXPRESS HER CREATIVITY.

"There's a lot that I want to create and accomplish as an artist. It can be really rough, but that's what made me who I am, so I'm grateful."

POPPY ROWAN

POPPY is the monarch of music at Rainbow High: bold, fresh, and creative. Poppy is the social butterfly of the group. Her tunes can set the vibe for any occasion.

FOCUS: Music Production

POPPY
MUSIC PRODUCTION FOCUS
RH

"Poppy Rowan, gettin'
the beats goin'.
My look is always
in rhythm.
My look is too fly."

#OMG POPPY HAS SOUND SYNESTHESIA— THAT'S WHAT IT'S CALLED WHEN YOU SEE MUSIC. SO SHE MAKES THE MUSIC SHE WANTS TO SEE!

#FIRE POPPY COMPOSED THE RAINBOW HIGH THEME SONG, "TURN YOUR COLOR UP."

#DYK WHEN POPPY CAN'T CONCENTRATE, SHE POPS ON HER HEADPHONES AND TURNS THE MUSIC UP!

SUNNY MADISON

SUNNY has such a happy outlook, it bubbles over to all her friends when they're together. Her quirky-cool style is the sparkle and gold at the end of her personality rainbow.

FOCUS: Computer Animation

SUNNY
COMPUTER ANIMATION FOCUS

#GOALS WHEN SUNNY WAS LITTLE, SHE PUBLISHED A COMIC IN *WINNERZ* MAGAZINE.

#FIRE SHE CREATED AN ANIMATED SERIES CALLED *HI HI KAWAII* BASED ON HER FRIENDS.

#FYI SUNNY JUST LOVES ALL THINGS ADORABLE, AND IT'S REFLECTED IN HER CUTE KAWAII STYLE.

#DYK SHE'S NOT JUST A FANGIRL, SHE'S A TRENDSETTER, TOO!

#OMG SUNNY'S 10TH, 11TH, AND 13TH BIRTHDAY PARTIES WERE ALL AT ESCAPE ROOMS.

#DYK SUNNY AND VIOLET HAVE BEEN BFFS SINCE PRESCHOOL.

"Animation lets me show the world I feel it and express it in a larger-than-life place where anything can happen."

JADE HUNTER

JADE

RH

COSMETOLOGY FOCUS

> "My biggest goal when I give someone a makeover is to give them enough confidence to be themselves, even when they take the makeup off. I practice that on myself every day."

#FIRE JADE HAS HER OWN MAKEUP LINE CALLED LOOK UP (BECAUSE THAT'S WHAT SHE TELLS HER FRIENDS WHEN SHE'S APPLYING THEIR MAKEUP!).

#DYK JADE CREATED A NEW MOOD MAKEUP PALETTE THAT REACTS TO HOW YOU FEEL.

#UMM JADE WANTS TO GET A THERAPY TARANTULA.

#LOVE JADE ISN'T JUST ALL ABOUT MAKEUP. SHE ALSO LOVES TO STYLE HAIR. HER ROOMMATES ARE ALWAYS BEGGING HER FOR HAIR MAKEOVERS.

SKYLER BRADSHAW

SKYLER is one of the most talented fashion designers at Rainbow High, but she prefers to let her work speak for itself. And it does. She's as sweet as she is stylish.

FOCUS: Fashion Design

SKYLER

RH

FASHION DESIGN FOCUS

"My rainbow is learning to take credit for my designs and to hear what people really think of my work. It's hard to put myself out there, but it's seriously making me a better designer and teammate every single day."

#DYK SKYLER IS SHY AND BELIEVES THAT ART ISN'T ABOUT THE CREATOR, IT'S ABOUT THE CREATION.

#OMG SHE DESIGNED A DRESS THAT *SIZZLE* CALLED "THE TOP SUMMER OUTFIT INSPO OF THE YEAR."

#DYK SKYLER KNOWS HOW TO DO BIRDCALLS.

#FYI SHE DOES NOT LIKE SURPRISES!

VIOLET WILLOW

VIOLET is a born diva who is camera ready 24/7/365. Her signature look is showstopping luxe pieces, but the real showstopper is her super-successful podcast, *The Vi Life*.

FOCUS: Digital Media

VIOLET
DIGITAL MEDIA FOCUS
RH

"I put a lot of my life online. It's a lot of pressure to be so on all the time, and it's definitely easy to lose track of real life, but my friends keep me grounded. They're my reality check, and my rainbow."

#FIRE VIOLET HAS WON MAJOR AWARDS FOR HER MAD PHOTOGRAPHY SKILLS.

#INFLUENCER *THE VI LIFE* HAD 500,000 FOLLOWERS WHEN VIOLET FIRST GOT TO RAINBOW HIGH, BUT IT QUICKLY GREW TO 600,000 AFTER HER FIRST FEW VIDEOS WENT MEGA-VIRAL.

#DYK VIOLET IS ALSO A REPORTER FOR *THE SCENE*, THE SCHOOL'S AWARD-WINNING MAGAZINE.

#CUTE VIOLET CALLS FANS OF HER PODCAST "THE VI HIVE."

AMAYA RAINE

AMAYA is all about being bold, like a rainbow. She dreams of one day setting fashion trends, and with her daring and unique style, she's already on track to live out her dreams.

FOCUS:
Fashion Design

AMAYA
RH
FASHION DESIGN FOCUS

©MGA

#OMG WHEN SHE STARTED RAINBOW HIGH, SHE HAD LONG, WHITE, GLITTERY PEEKABOO RAINBOW HAIR, BUT SHE LOVES TO CHANGE UP HER COLOR TO MATCH HER MOOD.

#FYI AMAYA DYED HER HAIR BLUE BECAUSE SHE SAID, "IT'S THE COLOR OF CALM."

#DYK AMAYA DIDN'T ORIGINALLY GET INTO RAINBOW HIGH, BUT WHEN A SPOT OPENED UP, SHE WAS PULLED FROM THE WAIT LIST AND JOINED THE TEAM.

"Sometimes I change my designs, and myself, so much I can lose track of the original. I'll seriously do anything to adjust things until people like them. So, I'm always working on keeping myself grounded and remembering what I'm made of: the whole rainbow!"

"Less talking. More working."

LOU WRIGHT

Headmistress

As the leader of Rainbow High, Ms. Wright is strict but fair, and her fashion instincts are always spot-on. She's always checking in on her students and gives really productive advice. Even if her criticism can be harsh sometimes and hard to hear, taking her advice makes us all so much better at what we do!

"With Grit, Love, Action, and Moxie, there's nothing you can't achieve here at Rainbow High."

#FYI SHE EXPECTS THE STUDENTS TO FOLLOW ALL THE RULES AT RAINBOW HIGH.

#GOALS MS. WRIGHT BELIEVES THAT THE RIGHT RUNWAY WALK BRINGS FASHION TO LIFE AND LIFE TO FASHION.

"It's time for za-zing!"

#DYK AT RAINBOW HIGH, MS. WRIGHT OVERSEES AN ELITE NETWORK OF SCOUTS WHO DISCOVER THE MOST EXCITING NEW TALENT TO ATTEND RAINBOW HIGH.

#FIRE MS. WRIGHT HAS EARNED A RAINBOW HIGH SCHOOL CREST PIN AND ENCOURAGES ALL STUDENTS TO SEEK OUT THE PIN FOR THEMSELVES.

"Rainbow High prides itself on challenging students to rise to the occasion."

> "A piece of clothing is only as good as its loosest stitch."

PAMELA MORTON

Advisor and Team Leader

Ms. Morton wasn't there to greet the new strudents on the first day of school this year, but she had an awesome excuse—she was at New York Fashion Week. Excuse accepted! Her role here at RH is to advise the first-years. She's also the team lead for one of the groups. She can be found setting up cool challenges that make her teams stronger, like a getting-to-know-each-other scavenger hunt and locking her group up in an escape room!

#GOALS SHE WENT TO RAINBOW HIGH, AND AFTER SHE GRADUATED, SHE BUILT A HUGE FASHION EMPIRE.

#DYK SHE LOVES A GOOD SURPRISE!

FOCUSES

Every student at Rainbow High chooses an area of focus for our studies. From the runway to the stage, from the screen to the page, we have worked together to put on some incredible productions.

But no matter what our focuses are, we're all focused on the four main principles of Rainbow High: **G.L.A.M.—Grit, Love, Action, and Moxie!**

- **Accessory Design**
- **Animation**
- **Art Direction**
  - Set Design
- **Computer Animation**
- **Cosmetology**
  - Hairstyling
  - Makeup
- **Digital Media**
- **Fashion Design**
- **Fashion Technology**
- **Graphic Design**
- **Journalism**
- **Lighting Design**
- **Mixed Media**
- **Music**
  - Instruments
  - Music Engineering
  - Songwriting
  - Vocals
- **Performing Arts**
  - Acting
  - Dancing
  - Singing
- **Photography**
- **Styling**
- **Textile Design**
- **Visual Arts**

RAINBOW

RH RH

FIRST-YEARS

name AMAYA RAINE

focus Fashion Design

look Rainbow · Bold, daring, and vibrant with gold accents

name BELLA PARKER

focus Art Directing, Set Design

look Pink · Classic big-city chic

name COLIN

focus Mixed Media

look Purple · Sporty casual

name DAPHNE MINTON

focus Accessory Design

activities Hosts a podcast about semiprecious stones called *Let's Rock*

look Sea-foam green · Gold accents and open-toed sandals

quote "Stay fresh."

name DARIA ROSELYN

focus Music, Songwriting and Vocals

look Pink and black · Roses and thorns make up her diva look

quote "Music speaks to me so you don't have to."

name EMI VANDA

focus Visual Arts

activities She's been known to paint with a latte to get the right color on the canvas.

look Purple and black

name GABRIELLA ICELY

focus Fashion Technology

activities Is also an inventor

look Ice blue · Snow and ice inspire her shimmery winter look

name GEORGIA BLOOM

focus Music

look Peach · Southern country style makes way for costumes when she's onstage

name JADE HUNTER

focus Makeup

look Green · Dramatic, comfortable, and bold streetwear

quote "This is me. Any questions?"

name POPPY ROWAN

focus Music Engineering

look Orange · Butterflies, shimmer, and glammed-out streetwear

name RUBY ANDERSON

focus Graphic Design

look Red · Casual and trendy with fire accents

quote "These shoes are FIRE!"

name SHERYL MEYER

focus Textile Design

activities Designs handbags

look Yellow plaid · Beverly Hills style

more
FIRST-
YEARS

name SKYLER BRADSHAW

focus Fashion Design

look Denim blue · Classic, down-to-earth, and imaginative

name STELLA MONROE

focus Cosmetology

look Hot pink · Posh and bling

quote "I fancy a bit of fabulous."

name SUNNY MADISON

focus Computer Animation

activities Creator of *Hi Hi Kawaii*

look Gold · Unique fabrics with bold details

name VIOLET WILLOW

focus Digital Media

activities Host of *The Vi Life*, influencer

look Violet · Showstopping luxury with bling

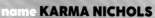

2

name KARMA NICHOLS

focus Digital Media

activities Host of *Kontent with Karma*

look Neon green · Glitter and shimmer

quote "It's not only about looking good; it's about doing good."

2

name RIVER KENDALL

focus Performing Arts

activities Music, football, former child star on the show *Lost at Sea*

look Turquoise · Sporty and casual

quote "That's so hype!"

3

name AIDAN RUSSELL

focus Art of Music

activities Prefect, reporter on the Rainbow High *Scene*, Fine Arts teaching assistant, and second-string quarterback on the Rainbow High football team

look Silver · Casual shorts, T-shirt, and high-tops with a sheer jacket

3

name AINSLEY SLATER

focus Fashion Design/Accessory Design

activities Prefect

look Purple and black · K-pop style with a striking ponytail

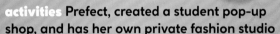

name **AVERY STYLES**

focus Fashion Design

activities Prefect, created a student pop-up shop, and has her own private fashion studio

look Shimmer · Unfussy and sparkling

quote "Always remember, the most important part of your outfit is confidence."

name **BRIANNA DULCE**

focus Animation

activities Installed a locker fan to get that "blowing in the wind" look. Created *Buenas Chicas*, an online animated series.

look Hot pink

quote "Life is sweet. Make the most of it."

name **KIA HART**

focus Styling

activities School matchmaker and runs the Rainbow Union

look Sparkle · Hearts and rainbows

quote "People are like shoes—they all have a perfect match."

name **KRYSTAL BAILEY**

focus Journalism

activities Editor-in-chief for the Rainbow High *Scene*

look Purple · Daring details with pops of silver

quote "At Rainbow High, we follow our creative dreams all day, every day."

name MARISA GOLDING

focus Photography

look Gold and black • Designer labels combined with unique styling

quote "Looking for that perfect shot."

FOURTH-YEARS

name CARMEN MAJOR

focus Music, Guitar

activities Songwriter and guitarist for the band Rainbow Dreams, Carmen used to attend a music conservatory and can play the cello.

look Fuchsia and hot pink

quote "There's nothing one-note about me."

name HOLLY DE'VIOUS

focus Performing Arts

look Icy blue, teal, and purple

name JETT DAWSON

focus Fashion Design & Textile Design

activities Took time away to intern with textile designers in East Asia

look Black and white • Her signature outfit has a Sharpie-styled look, but she's all about the unique fabrics.

quote "I don't do fashion—I am fashion."

name **LAUREL DE'VIOUS**

focus Performing Arts

look Fiery red and orange

name **LILY CHENG**

focus Textile Design

activities Works at her family's textile company in Shanghai during the summer

look Red, black, and gold · Modern style meets tradition

name **LYRIC LUCAS**

focus Music, Vocals

activities Former child actor

look Black and white · Rock goddess

name **ROBIN STERLING**

focus Performing Arts

activities Host of the secret Slumber Party Society

look Turquoise · Old-world Hollywood style

name **VANESSA TEMPO**

focus Music, Drums

activities Drummer for Rainbow Dreams and environmental activist. Her dad is a famous drummer.

look White and blue · Mixes high and low fashion

quote "I follow the beat of my own drum."

KONTENT WITH KARMA

"Looking back on this year, I think about times when I was my best self and when I didn't let the drama get the best of me. My biggest accomplishment was my editorial on Lily Cheng of The Scene. *I love sitting down with artists and hearing about their work and what inspires them."*

THE VI LIFE

Violet Willow's online reality show where she spills the tea about what *really* happens at the number one visual arts high school! The Vi Hive has 600,000 followers, with viewers tuning in each week to get the behind-the-scenes scoop!

THE SCENE

Our award-winning magazine is headed up by amazing upperclassperson Krystal Bailey. This year's reporters include Aidan Russell and Daphne Minton, and we welcomed new members Karma Nichols and Violet Willow to the team!

HI HI KAWAII

It's cuteness overload with RH's very own animated series starring the likenesses of some of our first-year students. It's led by Sunny Madison, who created the series on her very first day in computer animation class. We can't wait to see where she takes this kawaii series next!

Legend says at the end of the rainbow, there's a pot of gold. But the truth is, it's something even more amazing. Only a chosen few with an eye for bold fashion and art can follow the rainbow to our colorful elite art school, where everyone learns to flaunt their true colors.

THE RAINBOW HIGH CREST

The story of the school crest is shrouded in mystery, but with a little help from Ms. Wright, Violet and Sunny were able to get the scoop and earn the crest for themselves! But they haven't told the rest of us where to find it. So take the challenge to see if you can find it, too.

#DEETS

THE OUTSIDE OF THE CREST REPRESENTS THE OUTSIDE OF THE RAINBOW HIGH STUDENT.

"At Rainbow High, everything's more than meets the eye. Everyone makes beautiful and unique art that is seen on the outside. But to be chosen to represent the Rainbow High crest, you must also embody the G.L.A.M. virtues on the inside." —**VIOLET WILLOW, FROM *THE SCENE***

From brightly lit showcases to hard-to-find secret spaces, there's more to Rainbow High than meets the eye!

THE ATRIUM Home to student lockers and the unicorn school mascot statue, the Atrium is the central hub of Rainbow High. Because of its location and size, it's the perfect spot for assemblies, announcements, and hanging out between classes.

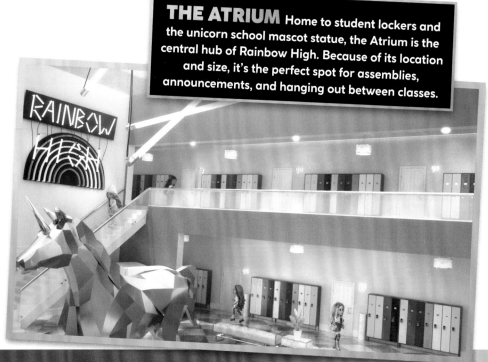

FASHION STUDIO Avery and Ainsley's fashion studio is where fashion magic is made! This space is so full-on inspiring, it's no wonder everything Avery creates is so FIRE.

Turn your color up, up, up, up, up, up, up, up

THE SALON The Salon is a cool space to try on new looks to find one that hits just right. And it's the coolest place to chill out in between assignments. Whether you want to stand out, try something new, or turn the color up, the salon is the place where Rainbow High students get a glow on.

THE AUDITORIUM

Whether it's a pep rally, runway, performance space, classroom, or school play venue, the auditorium always lets style take center stage.

BACKSTAGE *"My calling in life is set design. A fashion show is only as unforgettable as its catwalk."* —Bella Parker, first-year

THE CLASSROOM Sure, there are classrooms at RH just like any other school. They all look pretty much the same, although rumor has it that room 84 holds some sort of mysterious clue, but the only unusual object in that classroom is a hairdryer in the closet. So sus. We know!

"It hides in plain sight, but only those who seek it will ever see the light."

THE ARCHIVE A legendary secret space that contains the whole history of Rainbow High. According to Violet's article, a prize awaits anyone who can find it. Good luck, fellow students!

THE RAINBOW UNION
Sweet pastries, crafted teas and lattes, epic fashions, and a taste of inspiration.

Sparkle

When Ruby had her eye on some FIRE shoes, she tried to pick up some extra work (and extra cash AND a sweet discount) by helping out at the Rainbow Union. While she didn't top the charts in serving skills at first, her natural connection with the customers landed her the job.

The Rainbow Union is THE place where everyone spills the tea, and we're not talking about the drink. If you want to find out what's really going on behind the scenes at RH, head to the Union for a supersized serving of juicy gossip.

"This croissant is life-changing." —JADE

"The color and the texture of the latte are exactly what I was missing." —EMI

When Amaya spoke the forbidden phrase "Good luck," the runway run-through was cursed! The team formed a human pyramid to touch the unicorn horn and reverse the curse, but then—epic fail!—Amaya said it *again*! Sunny begged the fashion fates to take pity on their team, but the run-through was ruined and Ms. Wright was not amused.

In the end, the team turned their color up and made it happen!

NO RAIN, NO RAINBOWS

It didn't go smoothly for everyone, though. Gabriella got upset with Emi about missing her cue, and Ms. Wright pointed it out in their eval. Another team's set fell apart during the show, and they *all* got cut. Sooo sad!

"You've brought all your talents together and pushed yourselves to the limit."
—MS. WRIGHT

"That show was a complete joy to watch!" —MS. MORTON

Style! Swag! School Spirit!

Ms. Wright's cheerleading challenge was a big honor to bestow on Ms. Morton's first-year advisory team, and there was a lot of pressure to succeed. Two teams of upperclassmen had already failed!

We tried to focus on a uniform look for everyone, but Rainbow High students are meant to stand out, not blend in!

In the end, our signature styles were a big hit.

#oldschool

| 1970s | 1980s | 1990s | 2000s |

#newschool

It wasn't just the cheerleading outfits that got a makeover. Sporty hairstyles with bows and clips kept long hair neat and in place, while the makeup was super dramatic and totally FIRE! Face paint much, Jade? Loved it!

RAINBOW HIGH CHEER
"RAINBOW HIGH, GET READY, LET'S GO!
COME ON NOW, LET YOUR COLORS SHOW!
WORK TOGETHER, ALL FOR ONE!
CAN'T STOP US, WE'RE NEVER DONE!
TALENT, MOXIE, LOOKS SO FLY!
LET'S ALL CHEER FOR RAINBOW HIGH!
GO, TEAM!"

CREDITS:
Uniform design: Skyler and Amaya
Emblem: Ruby
Hair & makeup: Jade
Pom poms: Poppy
Cheers: Sunny and Violet
Judges: Ms. Wright and cheer squad members Karma, River & Stella

RH

RAINBOW HIGH™

Go, TEAM!

Rainbow High's football team made the playoffs for the first time in 20 YEARS! The entire school buzzed with excitement, and the pep rally was filled with extra pep and style.

When star QB Emerald McNabb sprained his ankle, we thought all was lost, but newbie Aidan Russell stepped in and stepped up to take our team to VICTORY!

RH

#aidan

WE WON!

45

CANDIDS AROUND CAMPUS

#attention

#chilling

#squadgoals

#memories

46

#doubletrouble

#yearbookvibes

RAINBOW
HIGH

#yum

#Agame

A Winter Tale of
Two Super-Beautiful Enchantresses

written by, directed by, and starring Laurel and Holly De'Vious

Laurel and Holly De'Vious made writer-producer-director-actor Rainbow High history with their stellar production.

Winter break at the Sparkle sisters' ski lodge was sprinkled with magic and drama when two enchantresses put a spell on a pair of ice skates.

Poppy and Sunny made their RH stage debut on ice.

Not only did Jade rock the stage styling, but she also saved the show as Georgia's understudy with her smooth skating moves.

CREDITS:
Sets: Bella Parker and Emi Vanda
Costumes: Jett Dawson and Gabriella Icely
Cast: Georgia Bloom, Poppy Rowan, Amaya Raine, River Kendall
Understudy: Jade Hunter

G.L.A.M. SLAM

First day of school—first challenge!

In the G.L.A.M. Slam scavenger hunt, the first-years followed clues that helped them get to know each other better.

CLUE 1:
Ruby's top seller

CLUE 2:
Bella's award records were the right combination to open the locker to retrieve the third clue.

CLUE 3:
Which of Violet's product sponsors held the next clue?

CLUE 4:
Sunny's lifelong bestie, Vi, led the team to the next clue about Sunny.

CLUE 5:

Skyler didn't want to brag, but she led the team to the fabric that got her noticed.

CLUE 6:

With time running out, the girls were almost stuck trying to figure out how Poppy's debut on the radio led to the next clue...

CLUE 7:

Jade's makeup line is called Look Up, and that's just what they did to find the final clue!

WINNERS!

A surprise awaited them back in the room where they started.

THE GRAND PRIZE:

A special gift for each girl to match their unique talents.

At the beginning of the year, the A's hosted a totally LIT party to celebrate and welcome the new students at Rainbow High.

Everyone was stressed to come dressed to impress at their first official event of the year.

Avery Styles invited the girls to a sneak peek into her Fashion Studio for style inspo.

The prefects invited Poppy Rowan to create a SICK playlist for the party and she totally rocked that challenge, turning up the beats for an EPIC celebration!

Despite some major drama (and a few sus moments that we won't mention), the party went off *almost* without a hitch.

Color Change Chamber

Amaya and Sunny discovered the style swap color change chamber secreted inside the salon. In a flash, Amaya's first fretful day at Rainbow High went from failure to fabulous.

Amaya noticed her new teammates were total pros at changing up their looks by swapping clothes, but when she introduced them to the color change chamber, they had the power to create legendary new looks with a push of a button!

"This is fire!"
—RUBY

"Totally sick—in a good way!"
—JADE

"Brilliant, Amaya!"
—SKYLER

"Big smiley!"
—SUNNY

"Living for this."
—VIOLET

"This transformation is a legend!"
—POPPY

THE GR8 HAIRSCAPE

Ms. Morton is always full of surprises. When she saw that her advisory team was having trouble getting along, she devised a plan that would make them work together—or else!

"Without teamwork, you're all toast."
—MS. MORTON

Ainsley and Avery led Ms. Morton's team to the salon and then locked them in! The only way out was to leave the drama at the door and cooperate.

"Be the rainbow. The strength of your group is the mirror of your success."

At first, things went smoothly. Colorful combs were the keys to reveal a lock combination.

But then the group got distracted when the door opened to reveal a stash of glowing beauty products!

Let's get glowing!

Time for a makeover!

Busted!

They failed the challenge, but all was forgiven since they did work together as a team, which was Ms. Morton's goal after all.

After Ainsley showed her in-progress Fashion Closet to some first-years, BFFs Ainsley and Avery barely spoke a word to each other.

That all changed when they each got an invitation from the legendary, secret Slumber Party Society.

"The sleepover is a sacred rite shared by friends throughout time, from sea to shining sea..." —ROBIN

"Stress levels can be completely bonkers at Rainbow High, and our society is here to remind us to have fun." —MARISA

"This is a time to reconnect as friends, not just classmates." —BRIANNA

The evening plans included rose-essence masks, slime packs, manicures, salty snacks, and a daring friendship pizza challenge, but bonding and spilling the tea were the real activities on the menu.

"Your opinion means the most to me, so it's the one I've been the most afraid of." —AINSLEY TO AVERY

RADIANT WEEK

Once every three years, Radiant Week takes over the school to celebrate the art of Rainbow High. We were challenged to showcase our out-of-the-box, show-stopping, and innovative high concept art pieces. We had one week to WOW a mystery judge, and we totally delivered!

PERSPECTIVE

Violet

Sunny and Brianna

Jade, Jett, and Robin

Bella, Sheryl, and Gabriella

Daphne and Amaya

Lyric, Carmen, Vanessa, Daria, and Poppy

Holly, Laurel, their assistant, and Avery

Ruby and Emi

NEWS FLASH DESPITE THE RUMORS SPREADING AROUND CAMPUS, RADIANT WEEK IS DEFINITELY NOT HAUNTED!

River and Georgia

THE DREAM TEAMWORK PROJECT DAY

A true marathon of the arts, the students had twelve hours to complete their assignments. Fourth-years led teams of first-years in an ambitious project.

Students had 12 hours to get a team project just right.

But while Rainbow Dream has mad skills at making epic music, they were an epic failure at making a group decision. Sunny came to the rescue, as team director, assigning roles and keeping everyone on deadline.

COLORS GO POW!

THE "COLORS GO POW!" VIDEO WAS A SMASHING SUCCESS!

"I THINK I CAN HANDLE POWY-WOW-ZOW." —EMI

"IT'S A DREAM COME TRUE." —DARIA

"WE'RE FREAKING OUT WITH EXCITEMENT AND ALSO TERRIBLE FEAR!" —SUNNY

"NOTHING MAKES MY HEART RACE LIKE A GOOD DEADLINE!" —RUBY

RAINBOW DREAM
Rhythm royalty: Vanessa Tempo
Vocals: Lyric Lucas
Guitar: Carmen Major

LYRIC

VANESSA

CARMEN

TEAM MUSIC VIDEO
Wardrobe: Gabriella and Skyler
Set design: Emi and Sunny
Music and tech: Poppy and Daria

GABRIELLA

DARIA

SUNNY

POPPY

EMI

SKYLER

"I LOVE THIS CAPTAIN SUNNY ENERGY!" —POPPY

"WE HAVE FIVE HOURS LEFT TO MAKE ALL YOUR DREAM TEAMWORK PROJECT MUSIC VIDEO DREAMY-DREAMS COME TRUE AND WE'RE MAKING THEM COME TRUE ON TIME!" —SUNNY

63

DORM LIFE

Dorm life is so much fun! We live in suites, which means we share a common room with other kids in our grade and we each have our own rooms, too. The first-years live on the third floor, and when we're not in class or working on projects, we love hanging out together in our own space and in the salon!

"**More friends for us both!**"
—VIOLET

PREFECTS: AINSLEY, AVERY, AND AIDAN

"My makeup skills are so good, it's scary."
—JADE

"Custom kicks. It's what I do. One of the things I do."
—RUBY

RUNWAY GROUPS

Our runway groups are also our advisory groups. Ms. Wright called it "the team that will make you or break you this year."

CHECK OUT AVERY'S CLOSET!

A place for everything and everything in its place. Form meets function with good lighting and a clean workspace. If you're looking to spruce up your own space, spotlight your favorite creations like their dressed mannequin, some posters, or a pillow in a bold accent color.

THE COMMON ROOMS

The dorm common rooms are great place for kicking back or freaking out about deadlines and drama. From fashion emergencies to friend friction, this is our home base. And when a certain someone got homesick, we brought the beach to her!

DRAMA AND SUS MOMENTS

The time when Sunny, Poppy, and Ruby went to Ainsley's fashion closet without the rest of the team.

The time Ruby spilled an iced drink all over Ms. Wright at the Rainbow Union and she thought she'd lost her sweet server gig.

The time Laurel and Holly De'Vious convinced the first-years that Rainbow High was haunted by a stressed-out former student ghost during Radiant Week. (Of course, the first-years turned the tables and scared them back!)

Who sent Amaya and Ainsley secret invitations, and WHY?

That time during Radiant Week when Amaya and Daphne got their project reviewed by Ms. Wright. DRAMA!

When the Assistant wrote Rainbow backward on the school mascot—and had to clean it up himself. Why did he do it?

Do the fashion fates *REALLY* get angry when anyone says "Good luck"?

Is there *REALLY* a ghost that haunts Radiant Week?

Is Sunny Madison *ACTUALLY* Ms. Wright's daughter? If not, why did she call her MOM?

Violet and Sunny were BFFs since preschool and planned on rooming together, but in a totally sus moment, Vi ditched Sunny on the roommate request form so she could branch out and make new friends. Fortunately, the girls made up pretty quickly, and it all turned out sunny in the end! Not so sus after all!

When Bella got suspended for sending out a photo of her work in an internship application... how DID she get back in?

"Getting kicked out is not something I'm proud of. So when people start asking questions about how I got back in, I just let them believe whatever story they want, even a crazy one about aliens."
—BELLA

#OMG

Bella confessed that she had to commit to community service for the whole term and polishing the unicorn statue every weeknight, horn to tail, to prove she'd learned her lesson.

THE DISH

Let's see what the students have to say about each other...

JADE: **Sunny lights us up and keeps us positive.**

SUNNY: **Poppy's music has all kinds of textures, like this! She makes us feel everything deeper.**

POPPY: **Ruby pushes our boundaries and adds fire to everything she touches!**

RUBY: **Skyler seems quiet, but her talent's loud and strong. She inspires all of us.**

VIOLET: **Amaya's filled with huge ideas! She never gives up, and thanks to her, none of us will either!**

AMAYA: **Jade doesn't hide anything and always tells the truth. That's why a compliment from her means everything!**

POPPY: **Violet reminds us that if art's going to matter, it has to be seen and shared.**

POPPY: Art of Music is my favorite class. Visualizing sounds is *way* beyond.

ART OF MUSIC

AIDAN: Art of Music is where music and art collide. It's like you're painting and sculpting with sound.

SKYLER: Runway Class challenges me to speak up for myself and see my designs come to life.

VIOLET: Video Production. If life is art, then I want to be the ultimate artist. Anyone can record their life all day. I work hard to do it in a way that says something.

JADE: Cosmetology for sure. Great makeup can show the real you or make you someone totally new. It's like magic, and I'm a magician.

RUBY: In **Mixed Media** class, I learn how to make art out of everything. I'm learning to work in every medium and turn my colors up!

SUNNY: Animation class. There, I can create a larger-than-life world where anything can happen.

JETT: Art of Fashion. Fashion is meant to be seen by the world. And with every new outfit, we can make ourselves into living art, no matter what we're wearing.

AMAYA: Design. Quality materials, make bold materials, all about craftsmanship.

ART OF FASHION

For their first winter break, Bella left for a road trip to the ski lodge with her roommates, the Sparkle Sisters, and Skyler headed home while the rest of the roommates planned a super staycation.

Vacay started out like a dream, binge-watching baking shows, experimenting in the studio, and planning a big Winter Break Dance Party, but Poppy's first snow day turned to disaster when she stayed outside on her own while the others went inside for rainbow swirl cocoa.

#SOS

#teamwork

Jade kept her wits and formed a plan: Violet called for backup, Ruby, Violet, and Jade launched a rescue mission, and Sunny stayed to keep Poppy's spirits up. Who knew stiletto heels would help save the day?

WINTER BREAK

Rainbow High Students always dress their best, whatever the reason or the season!

WINTER

DANCE PARTY

ROCKING OUT

CHEER

EVERYDAY AWESOME

©MGA

Creating runway-ready hairstyles? Easy. Getting my styling victims to sit still when I'm working on their hair? That's the hard part!
I'm not one for gossip, but I was asked to spill the tea on how some of my favorite everyday styles come to life, so, here it is.

SAVAGE STYLES
BY JADE HUNTER

← **POPPY ROWAN:** Poppy parts her orange and peach waves in the center, then pulls one side back loosely, securing it just above her right ear with two clips. To fit with her butterfly theme, her hair clips look like monarch butterflies. So on trend!

JETT DAWSON: The right side of her straight hair is black while the left side is full-on rainbow, including her bangs! She pulls the top half of her hair up into a small bun and leaves the rest to cascade down her back.

STELLA MONROE: Her hot-pink high pigtails are totally cute and practical. Pulling her hair up keeps it off her face, and it takes almost no time to do. Her morning routine: wash, comb, make a straight part, pull each pigtail into an elastic band, check the mirror, and she's good to go!

VANESSA TEMPO:

Vanessa wears her signature rainbow-streaked micro braids pulled up into a high ponytail, with two face-framing braids pulled out of the pony on either side above her eyes. To hold her high pony in place, Vanessa takes three braids from the back beneath the ponytail line and winds them twice around the rest of her hair, securing the ends out of sight. She tops it all off with a vintage denim scrunchie, and then she's ready to rock and roll!

SUNNY MADISON:

Sunny doesn't mind spending extra time styling her locks in the morning to get the perfect mixture of cute and stylish. She pulls her golden hair into a combination of dumpling-shaped odango buns and twintails.

KIA HART:

Kia's quadruple-braid, double-clip style keeps her hair out of her eyes and leaves the rest of her wavy bubblegum-sherbet-colored hair free to cascade wherever it flows. She makes the braids by taking the hair just above the space between her eyebrows, separating it into four strands, and creating four separate herringbone plaits. She plaits the two center strands back down the center and secures the two outside bands with elastic. She secures the loose hair on either side of her forehead with two baby clips—one says LOVE and the other says XOXO. Sooo cute!

GEORGIA BLOOM:

The secret to Georgia Bloom's always-stage-ready long, cascading, peach-colored waves is keeping her styling routine super simple. She starts with clean hair, then, when it's dry, a little defrizz oil helps tame any flyaways. Next, she tucks the front strands behind her ears and adds gold and silver hair clips on each side. Mixing gold and silver—so daring, but it works!

GET THE LOOK

WITH AVERY STYLES

THE KEY TO MIXING PATTERNS & PRINTS IS KEEPING TO A MONOCHROMATIC COLOR STORY— AKA STAY IN THE SAME COLOR FAMILY. MIX IT UP, AND YOU CAN PUT TOGETHER INTERESTING AND BOLD NEW OUTFITS!

DON'T FORGET ABOUT THE FINISHING DETAILS. ADD A BOLD ACCESSORY TO YOUR LOOK FOR A LITTLE SOMETHING EXTRA.

Always remember: the most important part of your outfit is confidence!

STYLING AN OUTFIT WITH DIFFERENT
FABRIC TEXTURES IS A FUN AND EASY WAY
TO CREATE A STYLISH NEW LOOK! PAIR
DENIM WITH SATIN, SEQUINS WITH FAUX
LEATHER—THE OPTIONS ARE LIMITLESS.

FIRST-YEARS' SIGNATURE STYLES

RUBY ANDERSON

STREETWEAR CHIC

BACKWARD BASEBALL CAP

FIRE ACCENTS

RED

T-SHIRT WITH A RED "SPARKLE" LOGO

VINYL BUSTIER TOP

FLANNEL PLAID SHIRT

SPARKLE GEAR

HIGH-WAISTED SKINNY JEANS

HEELED SANDALS WITH CLEAR VINYL STRAPS

CUSTOM KICKS

POPPY ROWAN

HIP-HOP VIBES

ORANGE

MONARCH BUTTERFLIES

RH

VINYL BUSTIER TOP

CROPPED PUFFER JACKET

KNEE-HIGH STATEMENT BOOTS

DJ SPECS

SLIP DRESS WITH A SHEER OVERLAY

GOLD ACCENTS

"FOR FLYING"

83

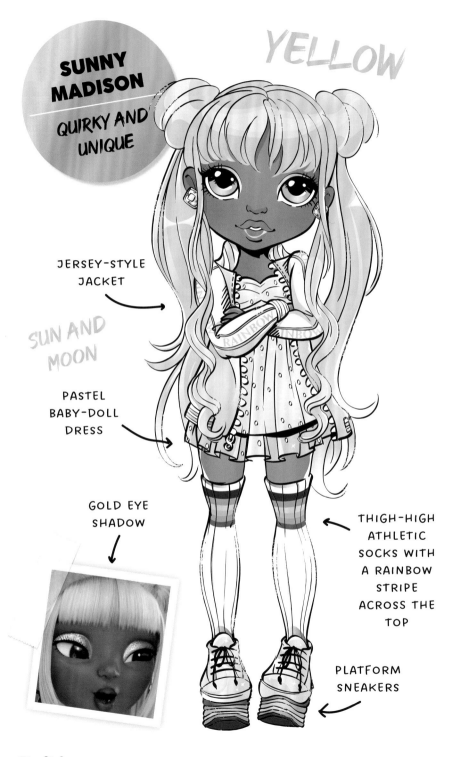

SUNNY MADISON

QUIRKY AND UNIQUE

YELLOW

SUN AND MOON

JERSEY-STYLE JACKET

PASTEL BABY-DOLL DRESS

GOLD EYE SHADOW

THIGH-HIGH ATHLETIC SOCKS WITH A RAINBOW STRIPE ACROSS THE TOP

PLATFORM SNEAKERS

JADE HUNTER

DRAMATIC AND BAGGY

GREEN

BEANIE

PUFFER JACKET

CASUAL

BAGGY T-SHIRT WITH LOGO

KNEE-LENGTH SHORTS WITH GRAFFITI

GRAFFITI

GREEN NAILS

SNEAKERS

85

SKYLER
BRADSHAW

ALL
AMERICAN

BLUE

DENIM
BUSTIER
TOP

CROPPED,
SHORT-SLEEVED
TURTLENECK

DENIM

DENIM
JACKET WITH
CHEVRON
STRIPES

CLEAR
VINYL BELT

DENIM
DRESSES

DENIM
MINISKIRT

UNDERSTATED

ANKLE
SOCKS

TRANSLUCENT
PASTEL
PLATFORM
SNEAKERS

VIOLET WILLOW

LUXE BLING

VIOLET

SHIMMER

GLAMOUR

SHIMMERY FAUX-FUR JACKET

IRIDESCENT SEQUINED HALTER-TOPPED MINIDRESS

VIOLET'S PHONE

SHIMMERY ANKLE SOCKS

PURPLE CHUNKY-HEELED SANDALS WITH PEARLS

BELLA PARKER

BEVERLY HILLS CHIC

PINK

PEARLS

BOWS

PINK CROP TOP

TWO-PIECE TWEED BLAZER AND MINISKIRT SET

PINK JACKETS

THIGH-HIGH SOCKS

OPEN-TOE SANDALS WITH CHUNKY HIGH HEELS

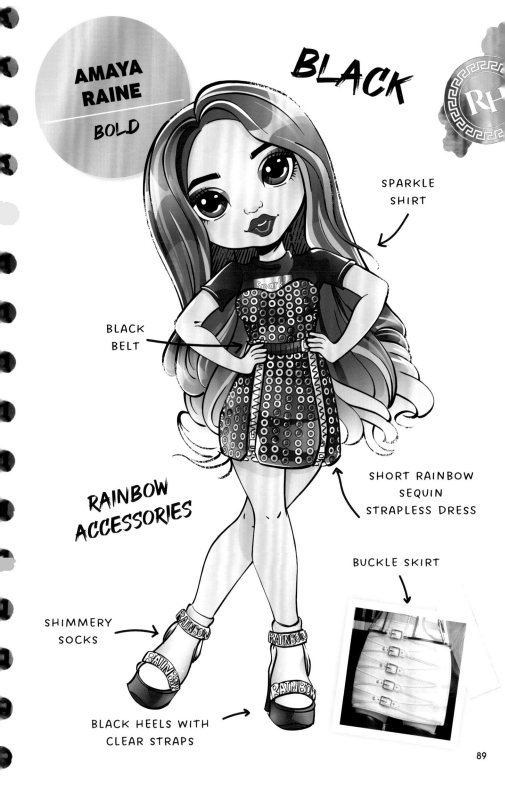

AMAYA
RAINE

BOLD

BLACK

RH

SPARKLE
SHIRT

BLACK
BELT

RAINBOW
ACCESSORIES

SHORT RAINBOW
SEQUIN
STRAPLESS DRESS

BUCKLE SKIRT

SHIMMERY
SOCKS

BLACK HEELS WITH
CLEAR STRAPS

LET'S ROCK!
BY DAPHNE MINTON

There's a lot of gold in the Rainbow High accessory rainbow, but there are also quite a few silver linings and colorful gemstones, too.

When adding accessories to your ensemble (that's fashion-speak for outfit), fashionistas look for statement pieces like the De'Vious twins' R and H earrings.

Some of us are totally team gold, while others are all about the silver.

ROCKIN' OUT AT RAINBOW HIGH
BY POPPY ROWAN

The music at RH is so fresh. I'm super psyched to write about the amazing and inspiring songs and musicians here.

This year, some of us got to work on a music video for the awesome student-run band, Rainbow Dream, featuring upperclassmen Vanessa Tempo, Lyric Lucas, and Carmen Major! It was a dream come true to help these amazing artists turn their color up.

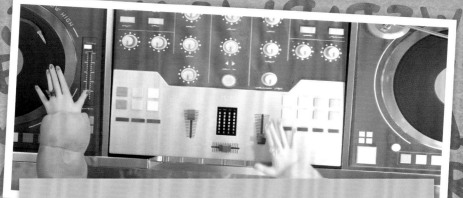

As for me, my signature music style is pop with sick beats mixed with EDM. I believe the right music can set the vibe for any situation.

The editors asked me to share the freestyle rap I came up with in class. I can turn anything into a song!

I LIKE THIS CUT AND I LIKE THIS STYLE
LOVE THE BEADING. IT'S SO SWEET AND I REALLY HAVE TO SMILE.
SKYLER, YOU'RE MY GIRL, SO I NEVER CRITICIZE,
BUT YOU'RE ASKING MY OPINION SO I'M GIVING YOU NO LIES.
IF I'VE GOTTA MAKE A CHOICE, I'LL JUST TELL YOU HOW I FEEL.
I SAY THIS ONE IS THE WINNER 'CAUSE THAT'S HOW I KEEP IT REAL!

Rainbow High is so awesome, we even have our own THEME SONG...
I dare you not to sing along to the chorus...

RAINBOW HIGH!

WHATEVER YOUR COLOR
YOU GOT A LOOK THAT HITS YOU RIGHT
JUST LIKE NO OTHER
YOU GOT THE HOOK SO AMPLIFY IT
TURN YOUR COLOR UP
TURN YOUR COLOR UP

GLOWIN'
SLAYIN'
FASHION
FRAME IT

RAINBOW HIGH!

Year in review spotlight: failures and successes

SUCCESS

Radiant Week

Rainbow High on Ice

Cheer Squad

Ruby on the cover of The Scene

Runway Week

FAIL

When Poppy got stranded on thin ice during winter break

When Georgia lost her voice right before the winter play

When Jade created mood makeup and Amaya's face turned beet red

Major freak-out when Amaya lost all the clothes right before the big runway show!

RH Sparkle

Social butterfly: Poppy

Most chill: Vanessa

Best matchmaker: Kia

MVP: Aidan

Most humble: Skyler

Biggest prankster: Ruby

Most outspoken: Karma

Most versatile: River

Best actor: Georgia

Boldest style: Jade

Biggest comeback: Bella

Most energetic: Sunny

Most likely to succeed: Krystal

Most comfortable: Marisa

How well do you know your classmates?

1. Which Rainbow High student was a competitive figure skater when they were younger?

2. Whose home is by the beach when they're not at Rainbow High?

3. Who spent the first few months of school at an internship traveling through Asia?

4. Which student grew up in a castle?

5. Who has a podcast about rocks & gems?

6. Which twin duo loves to create major drama onstage and off?

7. Which RH design student spends her summers working for her family's company in Shanghai, China?

8. Which RH Rockstar used to study classical cello at a music conservatory?

9. Who got kicked out for not following the rules?

answers: 1. JADE, 2. POPPY, 3. JETT, 4. STELLA, 5. DAPHNE, 6. LAUREL AND HOLLY, 7. LILY, 8. CARMEN, 9. BELLA

SEE YOU NEXT YEAR!